A Thought For

Robert E. Gilbert

Alpha Editions

This edition published in 2023

ISBN : 9789357947954

Design and Setting By
Alpha Editions
www.alphaedis.com
Email - info@alphaedis.com

Contents

A THOUGHT FOR TOMORROW

BY ROBERT E. GILBERT

Any intolerable problem has a way out—the more impossible, the likelier it is sometimes!

Lord Potts frowned at the rusty guard of his saber, and the metal immediately became gold-plated. Potts reined his capricious black stallion closer to the first sergeant.

"Report!" the first sergeant bellowed.

"Fourth Hussars, all present!"

"Eighth Hussars, all present!"

"Eleventh Hussars, all present!"

"Thirteenth Hussars, all present!"

"Seventeenth Lancers, all present!"

The first sergeant's arm flashed in a vibrating salute. "Sir," he said, "the brigade is formed."

Potts concentrated on the sergeant; but, aside from blue eyes, a black mustache, and luminous chevrons, the man's appearance remained vague. His uniform had no definite color, except for moments when it blushed a brilliant red, and his headgear expanded and contracted so rapidly that Potts could not be certain whether he wore a shako or a tam.

"Take your post," Potts said. "Men!" he shouted. "We're going to charge at those guns!"

"Oh, Oi say!" wailed a small private with scarcely any features but a mouth. "Them Russians'll murder us!"

"Yours not to reason why," Potts said. "Draw sabers! Charge!"

The ground quaked under the beat of twenty-four hundred hoofs. As the first puffs of smoke billowed from the entrenchments half a league away, Potts remembered that he had forgotten to give orders to the lancers. Should he tell them to couch lances, or lower lances, or aim lances, or—

"P. T. boys, let's go. Out to the door," a bored voice called.

Potts opened his eyes. He sighed. Again he had failed. The dayroom had hardly changed. The chairs were all pushed together in the center of the floor, and two patients with brooms swept little ridges of dirt and cigarette butts toward the door. Potts sat slouched in one of the chairs and raised his feet as the sweepers passed.

"Orville Potts, out to the door," the bored voice said.

Potts gave Wilhart a killing look when the big attendant, immaculate in white duck trousers and short-sleeved linen shirt, passed through to the porch. Potts wondered why so many of the attendants resembled clean-shaven gorillas.

He arose leisurely from the chair, shuffled around the sweepers, and entered the hall. A pair of huge, gray, faded cotton pants draped his spindling legs in wrinkled folds, and an equally faded khaki shirt hung from his stooped shoulders. Potts had not combed his hair in three days. He pushed the tangled brown mass out of his eyes and threaded between the groups of men that jammed the hall, smoking and waiting to go to the shoe shop, or the paint detail, or psychodrama, or merely waiting.

At the locked door to the stairs, Potts stopped and glared at the six patients already assembled.

"Hello, Orville Potts," said another long-armed, barrel-chested attendant. This one wore a black necktie, and, so far as Potts knew, had no name but Joe. Potts ignored Joe.

The attendant pulled a ring of keys attached to a long heavy chain from his pocket and unlocked the door, when Wilhart brought the rest of the P. T. boys.

"Downstairs, when I call your name," Joe said, and read from the charts attached to his clip-board.

When his name was called, Potts stepped through to the landing and descended the top stairs. Joe locked the door.

Potts looked up at Danny Harris, who stood motionless on the landing. While Joe weaved down the crowded steps, Wilhart took Harris by the arm and pushed him.

"Let's go," he said. "Here, Orville Potts, take Danny Harris downstairs with you."

Potts said, "Do your own dragging."

"Well!" Wilhart gasped. "Hear that, Joe? Orville Potts is talking this morning!"

Joe turned up a red, grim face. "He'll talk a lot before I'm through with him," he promised.

The sixteen patients from Ward J descended the stairs, were counted through another door, and formed a ragged column of twos on the concrete walk outside. With Joe leading and Wilhart guarding the rear, the little formation moved across the great grassy quadrangle enclosed by the buildings and connecting roofed corridors of the hospital.

Potts tried to close his ears to Wilhart's incessant urging of Danny Harris. Harris would do little of his own volition, but Potts was tired of acting as his escort.

The blue morning sky supported but a few brilliant clouds. Potts wished he were up there, or anywhere except going to P. T. He hated P. T. It terrified him. Potts closed his eyes.

Major Orville Potts stood in the soft grass and rested a gloved hand on the upper wing of his flying machine.

"Sir," he said, "with my invention, the Confederacy will soon put the Yankees to rout."

The general stroked his gray goatee and pursed his lips. Potts felt pleased that every detail of the general's uniform stood out in bold clarity. The slouch hat, gray coat, red sash, and black jackboots were more real than life. Of course the surrounding landscape was a green blur, but increased concentration would clear that.

The general said, "Ah'm doubtful, Majah. Balloons, Ah undahstand. Hot aiah natuahlly rises, but this contraption seems too heavy to fly."

"No heavier, in proportion, than a kite, sir," Potts explained.

The crude mountaineer captain, standing slightly behind the general, snickered.

"Hit won't work nohow," he predicted. "Jist like that there Williams repeatin' cannon at Seven Pines. Ain't even got no steam engine fur as I kin see."

Potts said, "This is a new type engine. It operates on a formula of my own, which I have named gasoline. Now, if you gentlemen will excuse me, I shall proceed with the demonstration."

Potts climbed into the cockpit. A touch of the starter set the 1,000 h.p. radial engine roaring. He waved to the gaping officers and opened the throttle. The bi-plane whisked down the field and rocketed into the blue morning sky.

Too late, Potts saw the buzzard soaring dead ahead. He shoved the stick forward, but the black bird rushed toward his face in frightening magnification.

Potts opened his eyes. He had walked into a wall.

"What's the matter, Orville Potts?" Joe asked. "You sleep-walking? Get in there! I'll wake you up."

Joe shoved Potts through the door marked PHYSICAL THERAPY and into the dressing room. With sixteen patients in the process of disrobing, the small room presented a scene of wild, indecent activity. Potts squirmed through the thrashing tangle to a bench against the wall. He sat down and removed a shoe.

Potts almost felt the currents surging through the neurons of his brain and sensed a throbbing on the inside of his skull. Twice this morning, he had tried to break through the physical barrier and had failed. Even with a minimum of thought, the reasons for failure became obvious.

Lack of intimate detail seemed the principle cause. In his attempt to reach the Crimean War and lead the Charge of the Light Brigade, he had been hampered by his ignorance of correct uniforms and commands. He did not know at what time of day the charge had taken place, the weather conditions, the appearance of the terrain, or even the exact date. He believed it was about 1855, but he wouldn't risk a dime bet on his guess. Perhaps an attempt to return to the past was certain to fail. Surely the past had happened, was settled, inviolate. Someone named Lord Cardigan, not Orville, Lord Potts, had led the charge.

Inventing an airplane during the Civil War also had no chance of success. No such thing actually happened, and, if it had, the plane would have been more crude than the Wright brothers' machine. Furthermore, Potts was no aviator. Success, if any, lay in the future. The future was yet to come, and Potts could mold events to his liking. Or perhaps he could move his body in space, instead of time. He could think himself out of the hospital.

"Orville Potts, get those clothes off!" Wilhart ordered. Potts slowly removed his faded garments. He took his place at the end of the line of naked men leading to the needle shower.

Joe stood in all his glory at what Potts called the P. T. machine. The apparatus was a marble box with rows of knobs and gauges and a pair of rubber hoses on the top. Potts felt sure that Joe took a sadistic delight in his work. As the line moved forward, he glanced at the attendant's florid face, tight smiling lips and squinted eyes. Potts shuddered.

No member of the hospital staff had ever condescended to explain to Potts the exact purpose of the P. T. bath, other than that it would make him feel good. It only frightened Potts. The correct procedure was that the patient stepped between the pipes of the needle shower and washed himself. Then the attendant turned off the shower and sluiced the patient with powerful streams of water from the hoses.

The routine seemed senseless and innocent enough, but Potts had heard whispered conversations in the night that filled him with horror. The P. T. machine, rumor said, was actually an instrument of torture and death. The water pressure could be increased to two thousand pounds, enough to push out a man's eyes or break his bones. Instead of water, the hoses could spit fire like a flamethrower. Acid could spray from the shower. Potts had even heard that Joe had killed seven men in the P. T. bath. How much of this was true, Potts did not know. When he saw bodies turn suddenly red under a rain of hot water, or writhe and tremble as if being whipped, he could believe all of it.

The line advanced slowly, like a gang of criminals going to the gas chamber. Potts grimly determined to think himself out of the hospital at once, for who knew when fire instead of water would spout from the hoses? If he recalled some place outside, in exact detail, Potts knew he could become all mind and project himself there. He must recall everything, scents, temperature, the ground beneath his feet, precise colors. Potts concentrated.

He tried to remember the home he had not seen for three months. He received a dim impression of a tiny crowded apartment and a wife growing increasingly indifferent. He could not even remember the color of her eyes, or whether the living room contained one easy chair or two. He would have to project himself to another place, one that did not seem like a vague dream.

Potts saw that his bath would come next. Danny Harris stood in the spray and stared stupidly at the tile floor. Potts looked at Joe. A wide smile that revealed two gold teeth creased the burly attendant's face. Hairy hands turned off the needle shower, twisted two more knobs, and picked up the twin hoses. Joe stood like the villain in a Western movie, blazing away with two guns, and shot thin powerful streams of water against Harris's spine. Harris shrieked, though he rarely uttered a sound outside the P. T. bath. As the icy water raked him from head to heels, he yelled and danced.

"Turn around," Joe commanded.

Harris pivoted and wailed, and Joe basted him on all sides with water. Potts watched fascinated as the thin body turned alternately blue with cold and red under the stinging water. He would not endure that again this morning. He knew now one place he could sense and visualize in complete detail.

"All right," said Joe, laying down his hoses. "Let's go, Orville Potts!"

Harris reeled, like a man rescued from drowning, into the dressing room, and Potts took his place between the four vertical pipes of the needle shower. From innumerable holes in the pipes, powerful jets of water spouted against his body. He stood with his back turned to the machine and made no attempt to wash. He never did—he saw no point in bathing without soap.

Potts thought of the Ward J dayroom, the room in which he had spent much of his time for the past three months. He visualized the maroon chairs with metal arms and legs, the green cretonne curtains, the cream walls, the black-and-red inlaid linoleum floor glinting with spots of old wax. He sensed a stale odor of tobacco smoke, furniture polish, and perspiration. He heard the talk of patients engaged in perpetual games of rook. He felt his thighs, hips, and back pressing against one of the chairs, and his feet on the smooth floor.

"Now, Orville Potts," Joe jeered, "let's hear you sing like Danny Harris!"

But Potts wasn't there.

Potts opened his eyes. He had always wondered how it would feel, but he had felt nothing. In the same instant, he stood tensed, waiting for the water, and he sat in a chair in the Ward J dayroom. Directly in front of him, a nurse played rook with three of the patients grouped around a square table. Not many patients were in the room at this hour, and no attendant stood guard. The nurse turned her head slightly. She gasped, shoved back her chair and ran to the porch. Nasen, the ward attendant, charged through the door she had used.

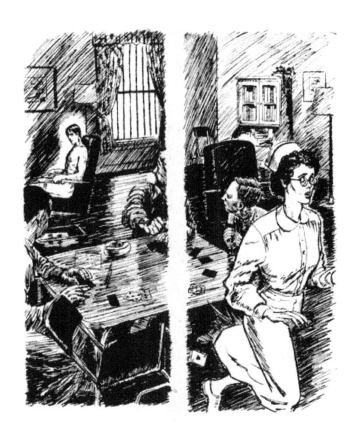

"Orville Potts!" he cried. "Where's your clothes?"

Potts then noticed that he was completely naked and wet.

Nasen dragged Potts from the chair, applied a light hammerlock, and marched his captive from the room. "Did you come over here from P. T. like that?" he asked. "How'd you get out?"

Potts went along willingly enough, but without answering.

Nasen unlocked the door to the shower room and thrust Potts within. "Stay right there," he said. As he was locked in, Potts heard the attendant call, "Frank, go tell Dr. Bean that Orville

Potts slipped out of P. T. with no clothes on. I don't know how. He must have stolen a key."

Potts took a towel from the shelf, sat on the bench, and rubbed his hair with the towel. He hoped they all went batty trying to learn how he had escaped. He thought most of the attendants should be patients anyhow.

Clutching a pile of clothing and a pair of slippers, Nasen returned. "Put these on," he said. "Orville Potts, you're in trouble now. What did you do with the key?"

Potts struggled into a tight blue shirt minus most of the buttons. "I didn't have a key."

"You're *talking?*"

"I can talk when I want to," Potts admitted. "I just never want to."

Nasen said, "That's more words than I've heard from you all at one time. Why did you come back stark naked like that?"

"I thought my way out," Potts explained, pulling on the trousers that had evidently been tailored for a giant.

"Oh, you thought your way out. Put those slippers on."

Joe and Wilhart, flushed and panting, charged into the shower room.

"There he is! Grab him!" Joe yelled. He seized Potts' arms and pulled them behind in a brutal double hammerlock.

"He's not giving any trouble," Nasen said. "What happened, Joe?"

"Damn if I know. He was in the shower, and I turned my head for a second. Next thing I knew, he was gone. What'd you find on him—a key or a lock-pick or something like that?"

Nasen grinned. "He didn't have even that much on when I first saw him. He came into the day room and sat down, and Miss Davis like to threw a fit."

Wilhart tossed a bundle on the floor. "There's nothing in his own clothes but a pack of cigarettes."

"Where's the key, Orville Potts?" Joe grated, squeezing Potts's arms. "You know what's going to happen to you? You'll get the pack room, or maybe Ward D. How would you like Ward D, Orville Potts?"

Nasen said, "If he had a key, he—"

"You better run along, Nasen," Joe said. "I think Dr. Bean wants to talk to you."

"Well, I—uh—" Looking worried, Nasen left the shower room.

Wilhart handed Joe a towel.

"Leave me alone!" Potts yelled.

Joe wrapped the towel around Potts's neck. "Where's the key, Orville Potts?"

"Help!" Potts cried. The towel tightened.

With rapidly dimming vision, he saw Wilhart assume a stance. A huge fist thudded against his shrunken stomach. He tried to scream, but the towel cut off all air and sound. Again and again, the fist struck.

Potts found himself sitting on the floor, gulping air into starved lungs. For a moment, he hoped he had managed another transportation, but the two white-clad human gorillas leering down at him proved he had not left the shower room.

"Get up," Joe said.

They dragged Potts to his feet. Nasen opened the door, clamped his teeth, and then opened his mouth to say, "Dr. Bean wants Orville Potts. I'll—"

"I'll take him," Joe said.

Potts winced as spatulate fingers almost met through his biceps. His feet barely touched the floor of the corridor when Joe marched him to the office of Dr. Lawrence D. Bean.

———————

Dr. Bean, a thin bald man, sat behind a maple desk and peered at Potts over spectacles attached to a black ribbon. Joe shut the door and leaned against it.

"I've been hearing things about you, Orville," Dr. Bean said. "We'll have a little examination. Now, hold your right arm out straight, close your eyes, and touch the end of your nose with your index finger."

"Can't we do without the foolishness?" Potts asked. He sank into the chair beside the doctor's desk and gently rubbed his bruised arm.

The doctor looked slightly startled, but said, "I'm pleased to hear you speaking again, Orville. If you continue to talk to people, take an interest in your surroundings, write home, you'll be out of here very shortly."

"He choked me," Potts said, pointing a thumb at Joe. "He choked me with a towel, and the other one, that Wilhart, hit me in the stomach."

Dr. Bean's spectacles jumped from his nose and dangled by the ribbon. He focused a pair of bleary eyes on Potts and said, "You know they didn't, Orville. The attendants are here for your benefit. They would never subject a patient to physical violence."

Potts laughed for the first time since he was hospitalized. He said, "Why don't you ask me what I did with the key?"

"What did you do with the key, Orville?"

"Talk about monomaniacs!" Potts snickered. "You all have one-track minds. You can't think of any way I could have escaped without stealing a key. Is any key actually missing? Did anyone see me crossing the grass or coming through the halls? I'll tell you how I did it. Exactly how. You already think I'm nuts, so it won't matter."

Again, Potts pointed at Joe. "Laughing boy here can bear me out. He was about to whip me with his ice water, and I vanished. I vanished from the shower and materialized in the dayroom."

Dr. Bean replaced his glasses and grabbed a pad and pencil.

"That's right, Doc," Potts approved. "Write it down. I'm giving you a better break than you ever gave me. I've been in this hospital four times, and no doctor ever sat down and explained what was wrong with me, or tried to learn why. There was something about combat fatigue, whatever that is, over in Italy. Otherwise, I don't know anything. If I so much as raise my voice or break a dish at home, my wife has me shipped back here as dangerously psychotic, or psycho-neurotic, or something. Which makes it nice for her.

"And what do you do when I come back? You give me electric shock treatments and have your sadists whip me with P. T. baths, as if torture could cure a sick mind! Maybe there's nothing wrong with my brain. Maybe it's just different from yours, or this jerk's, if he has a brain."

"Never mind, Joe," Dr. Bean cautioned in a theatrical aside. "Just stand by."

Potts smiled and said, "Take it all down. Then you can check your notes and decide if it's schizophrenia, or catatonia, or psychasthenia, or what not. I know a little about mental diseases from reading, and I'll explain my theory the best I can."

Potts tapped his forehead with a forefinger and asked, "What is a brain? You'll say it's an organ occupying the skull and forming the center of the nervous system, and the seat of intellect, or some such thing. I don't think so. It generates electricity. You know that. A nerve impulse is a wave of electricity started and conducted by a nerve cell. You can test it. You've made brain-wave patterns of some of the boys in the ward.

"The brain transforms energy into thought, or thought into energy. I'm sitting here thinking and not moving my body at all. My brain is transforming electric energy into thought. You're writing, and your thoughts guide the movement of your hand. Thought into energy."

Dr. Bean turned a page and continued to scribble rapidly. Potts heard Joe move and felt the big attendant's presence behind his chair.

Potts said, "The ability to think improves with use, like a muscle growing stronger with use. The first time you memorize a poem, it's a hard job. If you keep on memorizing, it becomes easier, until you read a poem a couple of times and you have it. The same goes for remembering. I'll bet you can't even remember how your breakfast tasted and smelled this morning. Probably not even what you ate.

"I practice remembering with all the senses. How things look and taste and smell. Exact colors, shadows, size, impressions. Think of an airplane, and you probably think of a little silver thing in the sky. Actually, an airplane is much bigger than that, so your mental picture of an airplane is all wrong. An airplane gives me a certain impression. I have it only when looking at one. Maybe it's an unrecognized sense. I have an entirely different impression when I'm looking at a horse."

Dr. Bean threw down his pencil, caught his falling glasses, drew a handkerchief from his breast pocket, and polished them.

"Too deep for you, Doc?" Potts inquired. "Well, just assume that my brain is a more powerful generator and transformer than any you ever saw. I've developed it by memorizing, remembering, visualizing, working problems in my head, and so on. I've been trying to make my brain take complete control of my body. The body is composed of atoms, and the atoms are electrical charges, protons and electrons. Therefore, you're nothing but electricity in the shape of a man.

"By changing myself to pure thought, or pure electricity, I believed that I could escape to the past. Get away from this age where a man is suspected of insanity if he so much as mislays his checkbook or kicks his dog. People didn't used to be crazy unless they went around hacking their relatives with an ax.

"I tried to meet Columbus when he rowed ashore from the *Santa Maria*. I tried to watch the Battle of Bunker Hill. I tried to lead the Charge of the Light Brigade. I tried to invent an airplane during the Civil War. I always failed, because I didn't have enough sensory knowledge of the period, and I couldn't change the past.

"I succeeded in P. T. because I transported myself through space instead of time. I knew every detail of the day room, so it worked. My brain reduced my body to its elemental charges in the P. T. bath and reassembled it in the dayroom. Something like radio, with the brain acting as sending set and receiver. Maybe we should call it philosophy, Doc. What is reality? If I sit here in your office but imagine I'm sitting in the dayroom, until the chair in the dayroom becomes more real than this, where am I actually sitting?"

Dr. Bean stood up, adjusted his glasses, and said, "Orville, I am going to do as you asked. I am going to tell you exactly what is wrong with you. You are suffering from distorted perception—illusions and hallucinations, disorientation. You are also becoming an exhibitionist and are developing a persecution complex. I thought, when you first came in, that you had improved. But if you don't pull yourself together and try to get well, you'll be in here a long time."

Potts's chair overturned as he thrust himself up. He placed his thin hands on the desk and said, "You psychiatrists can't see an inch in front of your nose! All you can do is quote a textbook. If anybody mentions mental telepathy, or predicting the future, or a sense of perception, you classify them as insane. You think you've reduced the mind to a set of rules, but you're still in kindergarten! I'll prove every word I said! I'll vanish into the future! I can't change the past, but the future hasn't happened yet! I can imagine my own!"

Joe grabbed the fist that Potts shook under the doctor's nose and pinned the patient's arms behind his back.

"Take him upstairs to Ward K, Joe," Dr. Bean said. "To the pack room. That should calm him."

"So long, moron!" Potts called.

"Let's go, Orville Potts," Joe said. "We're going to fix you up just like an ice cream soda."

"You won't pack me in ice," Potts promised. His thin body twisted in pain.

He closed his eyes tight and concentrated.

Joe's great hands clamped into fists when Potts disappeared.

———

Potts opened his eyes. He lay face down on a padded acceleration couch with broad straps across his brawny back and legs. Before his face, a second hand swept around a clock toward a red zero. Potts twisted his head slightly in the harness and looked at the beautiful young woman strapped to the couch on his right. A shrieking warning siren blared through the spaceship.

The woman smiled.

"Hia, ked," she said in strange new accents. "Secure your dentures. Next stop, Alpha Centaurus!"